Perseus

and the
Snake Monster

First published in 2008 by
Franklin Watts
338 Euston Road
London
NW1 3BH

Franklin Watts Australia
Level 17/207 Kent Street
Sydney
NSW 2000

Text © Karen Wallace 2008
Illustration © Jane Cope 2008

A CIP catalogue record for this book is available
from the British Library.

ISBN 978 0 7496 7993 4 (hbk)
ISBN 978 0 7496 8001 5 (pbk)

Series Editor: Melanie Palmer
Series Advisor: Dr Barrie Wade
Series Designer: Peter Scoulding

Printed in China

Franklin Watts is a division of
Hachette Children's Books,
an Hachette Livre UK company
www.hachettelivre.co.uk

Perseus

and the
Snake Monster

by Karen Wallace and Jane Cope

W

FRANKLIN WATTS
LONDON•SYDNEY

Perseus lived with his mother
on an island called Seriphos.

The king of Seriphos was a bully. He wanted to marry Perseus' mother. But she hated the king.

"Leave my mother alone,"
Perseus told the king.

"I will only leave her alone if you prove you're a hero," said the king. "What must I do?" asked Perseus.

"Bring me the head of Medusa,"
said the king, knowing it was
an impossible task.

Medusa was a monster with snakes for hair and teeth like a tiger's. Anyone who looked at her face turned into stone!

The goddess Athena decided to
help Perseus. She gave him a
shield that shone like a mirror.

"Don't ever look at Medusa's face," said Athena. "Only look at her reflection. Use this shield."

Then Hermes, messenger of the gods, gave Perseus a sword.

"Use this to kill Medusa," he said.

"Now you must go to see the
three witch sisters, to find out
where Medusa lives."

The three witch sisters shared one eye and one tooth. At first they refused to help. So Perseus snatched their eye and their tooth.

"Give us back what is ours!"
screamed the sisters. "Then we
will help you." Perseus agreed.

In return, they told Perseus where
to find Medusa. "But you'll need
more than that to win!" they said.

One sister gave Perseus
sandals with wings.
"You can fly high
with these," she said.

"And this helmet will make you invisible," said the second sister. Perseus was very pleased.

"Take this too," said the third
sister. "You'll need it." She gave
Perseus an empty sack.

Perseus flew into the night on his
winged sandals. No one saw him
with his invisible helmet on.

Perseus found Medusa snoring in a cave. The snakes on her head were hissing.

On the floor inside the cave he saw many heroes. They had all been turned to stone.

Perseus remembered what Athena had told him. He looked only at Medusa's reflection in his shield.

With one blow, he cut off her head
and put it into the sack. He was
careful not to look at her face.

Perseus returned to Seriphos.

"Let my mother go!" he demanded.

"Never!" cried the king, angrily.

So Perseus held up Medusa's
head and turned the wicked
king into stone.

Everyone on the island cheered.

They held a great feast for Perseus.

After that day, Perseus was
famous. He was the hero who
killed Medusa the Snake Monster.

31

Hopscotch has been specially designed to fit the requirements of the Literacy Framework. It offers real books by top authors and illustrators for children developing their reading skills. There are 63 Hopscotch stories to choose from:

Marvin, the Blue Pig
ISBN 978 0 7496 4619 6

Plip and Plop
ISBN 978 0 7496 4620 2

The Queen's Dragon
ISBN 978 0 7496 4618 9

Flora McQuack
ISBN 978 0 7496 4621 9

Willie the Whale
ISBN 978 0 7496 4623 3

Naughty Nancy
ISBN 978 0 7496 4622 6

Run!
ISBN 978 0 7496 4705 6

The Playground Snake
ISBN 978 0 7496 4706 3

"Sausages!"
ISBN 978 0 7496 4707 0

Bear in Town
ISBN 978 0 7496 5875 5

Pippin's Big Jump
ISBN 978 0 7496 4710 0

Whose Birthday Is It?
ISBN 978 0 7496 4709 4

The Princess and
the Frog
ISBN 978 0 7496 5129 9

Flynn Flies High
ISBN 978 0 7496 5130 5

Clever Cat
ISBN 978 0 7496 5131 2

Moo!
ISBN 978 0 7496 5332 3

Izzie's Idea
ISBN 978 0 7496 5334 7

Roly-poly Rice Ball
ISBN 978 0 7496 5333 0

I Can't Stand It!
ISBN 978 0 7496 5765 9

Cockerel's Big Egg
ISBN 978 0 7496 5767 3

How to Teach a Dragon Manners
ISBN 978 0 7496 5873 1

The Truth about those
Billy Goats
ISBN 978 0 7496 5766 6

Marlowe's Mum and
the Tree House
ISBN 978 0 7496 5874 8

The Truth about
Hansel and Gretel
ISBN 978 0 7496 4708 7

The Best Den Ever
ISBN 978 0 7496 5876 2

ADVENTURES

Aladdin and the Lamp
ISBN 978 0 7496 6692 7

Blackbeard the Pirate
ISBN 978 0 7496 6690 3

George and the Dragon
ISBN 978 0 7496 6691 0

Jack the Giant-Killer
ISBN 978 0 7496 6693 4

TALES OF KING ARTHUR

1. The Sword in the Stone
ISBN 978 0 7496 6694 1

2. Arthur the King
ISBN 978 0 7496 6695 8

3. The Round Table
ISBN 978 0 7496 6697 2

4. Sir Lancelot and
the Ice Castle
ISBN 978 0 7496 6698 9

TALES OF ROBIN HOOD

Robin and the Knight
ISBN 978 0 7496 6699 6

Robin and the Monk
ISBN 978 0 7496 6700 9

Robin and the Silver Arrow
ISBN 978 0 7496 6703 0

Robin and the Friar
ISBN 978 0 7496 6702 3

FAIRY TALES

The Emperor's New Clothes
ISBN 978 0 7496 7421 2

Cinderella
ISBN 978 0 7496 7417 5

Snow White
ISBN 978 0 7496 7418 2

Jack and the Beanstalk
ISBN 978 0 7496 7422 9

The Three Billy Goats Gruff
ISBN 978 0 7496 7420 5

The Pied Piper of Hamelin
ISBN 978 0 7496 7419 9

Goldilocks and the
Three Bears
ISBN 978 0 7496 7903 3

Hansel and Gretel
ISBN 978 0 7496 7904 0

The Three Little Pigs
ISBN 978 0 7496 7905 7

Rapunzel
ISBN 978 0 7496 7906 4

Little Red Riding Hood
ISBN 978 0 7496 7907 1

Rumpelstiltskin
ISBN 978 0 7496 7908 8

HISTORIES

Toby and the Great Fire of
London
ISBN 978 0 7496 7410 6

Pocahontas the Peacemaker
ISBN 978 0 7496 7411 3

Grandma's Seaside Bloomers
ISBN 978 0 7496 7412 0

Hoorah for Mary Seacole
ISBN 978 0 7496 7413 7

Remember the 5th
of November
ISBN 978 0 7496 7414 4

Tutankhamun and the Golden
Chariot
ISBN 978 0 7496 7415 1

MYTHS

Icarus, the Boy Who Flew
ISBN 978 0 7496 7992 7 *
ISBN 978 0 7496 8000 8

Perseus and the
Snake Monster
ISBN 978 0 7496 7993 4 *
ISBN 978 0 7496 8001 5

Odysseus and the
Wooden Horse
ISBN 978 0 7496 7994 1 *
ISBN 978 0 7496 8002 2

Persephone and the
Pomegranate Seeds
ISBN 978 0 7496 7995 8 *
ISBN 978 0 7496 8003 9

Romulus and Remus
ISBN 978 0 7496 7996 5 *
ISBN 978 0 7496 8004 6

Thor's Hammer
ISBN 978 0 7496 7997 2*
ISBN 978 0 7496 8005 3

No Dinner for Anansi
ISBN 978 0 7496 7998 9 *
ISBN 978 0 7496 8006 0

Gelert the Brave
ISBN 978 0 7496 7999 6*
ISBN 978 0 7496 8007 7

* hardback